The Adventures of Robin Hood

The Adventures of Robin Hood

A Traditional Family Pantomime
by Brian Luff

FIT2FILL

The Adventures of Robin Hood
This Edition published 2021 by Fit2Fill

(c) Copyright Brian Luff 2021

All rights reserved. No parts of this publication may be produced, stored in or introduced into a retrieval system, or transmitted in any form or by any means such as electronic, mechanical, theatrical or otherwise without prior permission from the publisher.

ISBN 978-1-716-12257-6

Licensing Information

This edition of *The Adventures of Robin Hood* is published by Fit2Fill to whom enquiries regarding licencing of rehearsal scripts and current royalty rates may be addressed. Telephone 0044 20 8340 9419. Email: mail@pantoscripts.biz

CONDITIONS

1. A Licence must be acquired for every public or private performance of this script and the appropriate royalty paid: if extra performances are arranged after a Licence has already been issued, it is essential that Fit2Fill be informed immediately and the appropriate royalty paid, whereupon an amended Licence will be issued.

2. The availability of this script does not imply that it is automatically available for private or public performance and Fit2Fill reserve the right to refuse to issue a Licence to Perform, for whatever reason. Therefore a Licence should always be obtained before any rehearsals start.

3. All Fit2Fill scripts are fully protected by copyright acts. Under no circumstances may they be reproduced by photocopying or any other means, either in whole or in part, without the written permission of the publishers

4. The Licence referred to above only relates to live performances of this script. A separate Licence is required for videotaping or sound recording of a Fit2Fill script, which will be issued on receipt of the appropriate fee.

5. Fit2Fill works must be played in accordance with the script and no alterations, additions or cuts should be made without the prior consent from Fit2Fill. This restriction does not apply to minor changes in dialogue, strictly local or topical gags and, where permitted in the script, musical and dancing numbers.

6. The full name of this script and the full name of the author shall be stated on all publicity, programmes etc. The programme credits shall also state "Script provided by pantoscripts.biz"

The Adventures of Robin Hood
A Traditional Family Pantomime by Brian Luff

LIST OF CHARACTERS

Robin Hood – Principal Boy

Maid Marian – Daughter of King Richard

Dame Dora – Robin Hood's mother

Sheriff of Nottingham – The villain of the piece

Little June – A quite tall woman

Friar Tuck – A very jolly monk

Will Scarlett – A chirpy chappie with a heart of gold

Denchman the Henchman – The name says it all

Juliet – Maid Marian's best friend

Alan a Dale – a traveling minstrel.

Mystic Reg – a psychic

Leafworm – A talking tree

King Richard – King of England

Long Face the Pantomime Horse – a pantomime horse

Plus, a lively bunch of villagers, children, castle guards and heralds.

SYNOPSIS OF SCENES

ACT ONE

Scene 1 The Village Square

Scene 2 The Sheriff's Castle

Scene 3 The Forest

Scene 4 A Gymnasium

Scene 5 The Sheriff's Castle

Scene 6 The Forest

Scene 7 The Castle Courtyard

ACT TWO

Scene 1 The Forest

Scene 2 The Castle Dungeon

Scene 3 Dame Dora's Artisan Bakery

Scene 4 The Forest

Scene 5 The Castle Courtyard

Scene 6 The Sheriff's Castle

ACT 1

Scene 1

The Village Square. Dame Dora, Juliet, the villagers and some children sing the opening number.

Song 1

At the end of the song, Denchman the Henchman enters.

Dame Dora Look out everyone, it's Denchman the Henchman! Personal assistant to The Sheriff of Nottingham and one of the most villainous men in all of Sherwood Forest!

The villagers all boo and encourage the audience to do the same.

Denchman the Henchman Be quiet you rabble! *(To Dora)* You!

Dame Dora Me?

Denchman the Henchman Yes you. Come here.

Dora skips over to him.

Denchman the Henchman I've warned you before, Dame Dora. If you don't show me some respect, I will confiscate your lands and throw you into the castle dungeons!

Dame Dora *(Flirty)* You wouldn't.

Denchman the Henchman I would.

Dame Dora You wouldn't.

Denchman the Henchman I would.

Dame Dora You would.

Denchman the Henchman I wouldn't.

Dame Dora Ha! Gotcha!

Denchman the Henchman Damn! I fell for it again.

Dame Dora *(To audience)* A bad man, but strangely attractive.

Denchman the Henchman *(Turning to audience)* Ladies and gentlemen and boys and girls, please welcome The Sheriff of Nottingham!

The villagers boo some more. The Sheriff enters, accompanied by two castle guards.

Sheriff Ah, good afternoon everyone! How delightful to hear your sweet, contented, happy voices. However, it is a pity that you are all so ugly! *(To the audience).* You could have at least made a bit of an effort. *(Picking out a man in the audience)* You! That man in the front row. When did you last iron that shirt? It's a disgrace! *(Picking out a woman)* And you! The lady in the third row. Have you never heard the word "hairdresser"? You look like you've been turned upside-down and used as a mop to clean the kitchen floor!

Denchman the Henchman Very amusing, your grace. Such a cutting remark.

Sheriff Don't grovel, Denchman.

Denchman the Henchman A thousand apologies, your grace.

Sheriff *(To all)* Right, pay attention peasants! It's time to talk about my very favourite subject?

Dame Dora Is it stamp collecting?

Sheriff No!

Dame Dora D.I.Y?

Sheriff No!!!

Dame Dora Is it Nottingham Forest Football Club?

Sheriff Silence, you insolent woman! Everyone knows that my very favourite subject is… tax.

Dame Dora Tax?

Sheriff *(Right in Dame Dora's face)* Tax!!!

Dame Dora Let me guess. You've decided to abolish all taxation?

Sheriff Ridiculous.

Dame Dora You're lowering the rate of VAT?

Sheriff Outrageous!

Dame Dora I've got it! You're giving us all a massive tax refund, in cash, and sending us on a free holiday to Skegness.

Sheriff Not quite.

Dame Dora Oh.

Sheriff Tell them, Denchman!

Denchman the Henchman *(reading from scroll)* The Evil Sheriff of Nottingham hereby decrees…

Sheriff Don't call me evil.

Denchman the Henchman *(reading from scroll)* The Sheriff of Nottingham hereby decrees that henceforth all taxes will be… *doubled!*

Dame Dora Doubled? That's not fair!

Sheriff You think so?

Dame Dora Yes.

Sheriff Very well. All taxes will be trebled!!!

Dame Dora That's even *more* unfair!

Denchman the Henchman *(Whispers)* Dame Dora, I wouldn't say anything else if I were you.

Dame Dora Right.

Sheriff *(To all)* While King Richard is out of the country I can set the taxes in Nottingham at any rate I like.

Villager God save the King!

Sheriff Who said that?

Silence.

Sheriff Come on, who was it?

Silence.

Sheriff Right. You are all going to stand here, with your hands on your heads, until someone owns up. Come on, hands on heads!

They all put their hands on their heads. Silence.

Sheriff I can wait all day.

Villager *(Reluctantly)* Sigh! It was me.

Sheriff Denchman, confiscate all of that man's property and throw him into the river.

Villager But, I can't swim!

Sheriff Then this would be an excellent time to learn.

The villager is dragged off by two castle guards. Offstage splash.

Sheriff *(To audience)* I do so love being nasty. Now, where was I? Oh yes. All outstanding tax must be paid by close of play tomorrow, and anyone who doesn't cough up the cash will be sent to the castle dungeons to have their toes nibbled by rats. Any questions?

Dame Dora *(Putting her hand up)* I have a question.

Sheriff What is it?

Dame Dora What year was the Battle of Hastings?

Sheriff Denchman, give that woman an on-the-spot fine and ban her from all public gatherings for 6 months.

Denchman the Henchman Yes, your grace.

Sheriff Farewell, peasants. Have a nice day!

The villagers and audience boo the sheriff as he exits with Denchman the Henchman..

Sheriff *(To audience)* Oh, shut up.

Maid Marian enters from the other side of the stage, followed close behind by her best friend Juliet.

Juliet Marian! Wait for me!

Marian *(to audience)* Hello everyone! I'm Marian. Has the Sheriff of Nottingham been here?

Audience Yes!!

Marian Which way did he go?

The audience point offstage.

Marian Then we need to go in the *opposite* direction.

Juliet *(Whispering to the audience)* Marion is trying to avoid the Sheriff. He has asked her to marry him.

Marian Oh, don't tell them that, Juliet! I can't stand the sight of the man. He's cunning, and wicked, and selfish, and greedy, and deceitful...

Juliet *(To audience)* Those are just his good points.

Marian And his eyes are too close together.

Juliet I've noticed that as well.

Marian I can't possibly marry the Sheriff! I have promised to marry... Robin Hood.

Juliet Has anyone pointed out to you that marrying an outlaw would be an extremely bad career move?

Marian Yes.

Juliet Who?

Marian Everyone.

Juliet Exactly.

Maid Marian I don't care! I love Robin with all my heart and I'm going to marry him.

Juliet Well, until you and Robin get hitched you'll just have to make do with being friends with me.

Song 2

Marian and Juliet sing a duet about friendship. At the end of the song...

Maid Marian That song has really cheered me up.

Juliet Good.

Maid Marian But the bad news is that the Sheriff has asked me to go and have dinner with him at the castle tonight.

Juliet Well, you can't turn him down. The Sheriff is a very powerful man. You'll have to go.

Maid Marian I know.

Juliet I've got an idea. Why don't you take a chaperone with you?

Maid Marian A chaperone?

Juliet Yes! Someone to make sure that you're not left alone with the Sheriff.

Maid Marian That's a great idea. But who?

Juliet I should have thought that was perfectly obvious....

Marian and Juliet run off. Dame Dora enters from the opposite side.

Dame Dora *(to audience)* Hello everyone!

Audience Hello!

Dame Dora I didn't get a chance to introduce myself before. What with all that mildly amusing banter with the Sheriff. I am Dame Dora, mother of Robin of Sherwood and future mother-in-law to the delightful Maid Marian. I run the artisan bakery in Sherwood. We make small cakes, tall cakes, big cakes, fig cakes and banana cakes. Coffee cake, banoffee cake, Eccles cake, speckles cake, cheesecake, Japanese cake and jam tarts. We also make the gooiest, chewiest, chocolate cakes you've ever tasted and the sourest sour dough bread in Nottingham. It tastes horrible but it's super expensive and all the all rich people pay a fortune for it. And of course, I run the Robin Hood fan club.

Dame Dora *(contd.)* It's hard work being the mother of a living legend you know. While he's out robbing from the rich and giving to the poor, I have to open sack-loads of his fan mail, send out signed photographs and moderate his Facebook, Twitter and his Instagram feeds. Some fans even want to buy his tights. I wouldn't mind, but they'll only buy them if he wears them first. Heaven knows what that's all about. And as if life wasn't tough enough, I've been married five times, divorced three times and I buried two of them. They weren't dead I just buried two of them. Ooh, I am sooo exhausted! I could really do with a bit of spontaneous sympathy. I *said*, I could do with a bit of spontaneous sympathy.

Audience Ahhhhhh!

Dame Dora Oh, come on. It's not like you haven't been to a panto before! I could do with a bit of spontaneous sympathy!

Audience Ahhhhhh!

Dame Dora That's more like it. *(Drying eyes with hanky)* I'm filling up here. Thank you all, every last one of you, for your support. I will wear it always.

Song 3

Dame Dora sings a song about being a sexy woman. At the end of the song...

Dame Dora Now, if you'll excuse me I must catch up with Marian. She's asked me for my recipe for fish finger and picked onion sandwiches. See you later!

She exits. Enter Will Scarlett with Friar Tuck.

Will Scarlett Hello everyone! I am Will Scarlett and this is Friar Tuck.

Friar Tuck Hello everyone!

Will Scarlett Friar Tuck is of course a friar.

Friar Tuck Which is a bit like being a monk, except that I deep fry everything.

Will Scarlett Which is the worst joke of the whole evening.

Friar Tuck I'm also in charge of Human Resources and Health & Safety.

Will Scarlett He checks to see that our arrows are not too pointy and our swords are not too sharp.

Will Scarlett We are members of Robin Hood's famous Merry Men.

Friar Tuck Oh dear, you can't call us the "Merry Men" anymore.

Will Scarlett Can't I?

Friar Tuck No!

Will Scarlett Why not?

Friar Tuck Because, Will Scarlett, in case you haven't noticed, there are men *and* women in our merry band.

Will Scarlett Are there?

Friar Tuck Yes. What about "Little June"?

Will Scarlett Little June? Who is Little June?

Friar Tuck You know, Terry's wife. Little June.

Will Scarlett I thought that was Little John.

Friar Tuck No!

Will Scarlett I must get some glasses.

Friar Tuck *(To audience)* Should have gone to Specsavers.

Will Scarlett Well, what *should* we call ourselves?

Friar Tuck Well the recommendation from Human Resources is that we call ourselves "Robin Hood and His Merry Men-*Slash*-Women"? *("Slash" is always emphasised with a large slashing motion with one arm).*

Will Scarlett "Merry Men-Slash-Women"?
Friar Tuck Yes.

Will Scarlett Ok. I'll give it a go.

Friar Tuck Start again.

Will Scarlett Hello everyone! My name is Will Scarlett and this is Friar Tuck, yadda, yadda, yadda. We are members of Robin Hood's famous Merry Men-Slash-Women.

Friar Tuck Perfect.

Will Scarlett We all live together in Sherwood Forest, which was recently designated a place of outstanding natural beauty.

Friar Tuck So we've got a English Heritage gift shop and a National Trust car park.

Will Scarlett It's freezing cold in the winter but the scenery's lovely and we don't have to pay any rent. Would you like to join Robin Hood's Merry Men-Slash-Women?

Audience Yes!

Will Scarlett Great! Here's what you have to do. Every time I come on I'll say "Hello Merry Men-Slash-Women" and you shout out ,"We're all very merry and we like cream and jelly!" Do you think you can do that?

Audience Yes!

Will Scarlett OK, let's try it. I'll go off and come on again.

Will quickly runs off and comes back on.

Will Scarlett "Hello Merry Men-Slash-Women!"

Audience We're all very merry and we like cream and jelly!

Will Scarlett That was rubbish! I could hardly hear you! Let's try that again.

He dashes off again and runs back on.

Will Scarlett "Hello Merry Men-Slash-Women!"

Audience We're all very merry and we like cream and jelly!

Will Scarlett Brilliant! Give yourselves a big round of applause!

Audience applaud.

Friar Tuck *(aside to audience)* Oh and by the way, you do *not* have to say you love cream and jelly if you are lactose intolerant.

Will Scarlett Health & Safety.

There is the sound of a horn playing a little fanfare.

Will Scarlett Heads up everyone! Sounds like the boss has arrived.

Robin Hood enters flanked by Little June, who is struggling to carry three big sacks. Villagers start to appear in the town square.

Villagers Hoorah! It's Robin Hood!

Robin *(To villagers)* Ssshh! I'm trying to keep a low profile.

Villagers Sorry.

Robin *(To villagers)* Isn't anyone going to ask me what's in these sacks?

Villagers *(all together)* What's in those sacks, Robin?

Robin I'm glad you asked me that. In these sacks are various items that have been stolen from the village by the Sheriff's men.

Villagers Hoorah!

Robin Little June...

Little June Yes Robin?

Robin Hand those sacks over to the villagers.

Little June I'll be glad to put them down. They weigh a ton!

Little June hands the sacks over to the villagers.

First Villager How did you get our possessions back?

Little June Well, we happened to be at the Sheriff's castle and they accidentally fell into our pockets.

Friar Tuck *(crossing himself)* Lord forgive us.

Second Villager *(opening sack)* Hoorah! It's my silver goblet!

Third Villager Hold on, that's *my* silver goblet!

First Villager No way! That goblet was stolen from *my* house!

Robin *(Aside to audience)* Methinks this might be a little more complicated than I thought.

Second Villager runs off pursued by First Villager and Third Villager.

First Villager Give me that goblet!

Third Villager Hand it over!

The other villagers grab the other sacks and quickly follow.

Robin *(Calling after them)* Don't argue! There will soon be enough silver goblets for everyone!

Robin runs after them.

Will Scarlett, Friar Tuck and Little June walk forward and the tabs close behind them.

Friar Tuck *(to Little June)* So, Little June, how is your husband Terry?

Little June Terry is very well. Thanks for asking.

Will Scarlett *(To the audience)* Terry and June. What are the chances?

Song 4

Tuck, Little June and Will Scarlett sing a song about friendship. After the song they exit.

Scene 2

Tabs open to reveal the Castle. The Sheriff and Denchman the Henchman are onstage. The Sheriff is looking into a big mirror.

Denchman the Henchman You called for me, your grace?

Sheriff Yes, Denchman. I want you to help me get ready for my dinner date with Maid Marian. She'll be here at any minute.

Denchman the Henchman What would you like me to do?

Sheriff I need some advice about my clothes.

Denchman the Henchman I'll do my best, your grace.

Sheriff Should I wear the crepe cape or the taupe *(pronounced "tope")* cloak?

Denchman the Henchman Mm. The crepe cape or the taupe cloak.

Sheriff Yes.

Denchman the Henchman I prefer the crepe cape, your grace.

Sheriff Are you sure?

Denchman the Henchman The crepe cape is more stylish than the taupe cloak. What are you wearing it with?

Sheriff A vest.

Denchman the Henchman Which vest?

Sheriff The vest with a crest.

Denchman the Henchman The crepe cape and the vest with a crest?

Sheriff Yes.

Denchman the Henchman What about that dark green, sleeveless, fitted shirt.

Sheriff The gherkin jerkin?

Denchman the Henchman Yes. I like the gherkin jerkin.

Sheriff The crepe cape, the vest with a crest and the gherkin jerkin?

Denchman the Henchman Very smart. What about the brown gown?

Sheriff The brown gown?

Denchman the Henchman Yes.

Sheriff I only wear the brown gown at weekends. With the shocking stockings.

Denchman the Henchman I've got an idea..

Sheriff What?

Denchman the Henchman Why don't you just wear the clothes you are wearing now?
Sheriff Good idea. You *are* a treasure, Denchman.

Denchman the Henchman Thank you, your Grace.

Enter a herald.

Herald The Lady Marian has arrived, your grace.

Sheriff Hand me that aftershave, Denchman?

Denchman hands the Sheriff a big bottle of aftershave. He sploshes it onto his cheeks. It stings.

Sheriff Ow, ow, ow, ow, ow, ow, ow!

Denchman the Henchman Are you alright, your grace?

Sheriff I haven't finished yet. Ow, ow, ow, ow, ow, ow, ow!

Herald Accompanying Lady Marian, Dame Dora of Sherwood.

Sheriff Dame Dora??? What's that awful woman doing here.

Enter Marian and Dame Dora flanked by two castle guards.

Dame Dora Well, that's a charming welcome I must say.

Marian Dame Dora is here as my chaperone.

Sheriff Chaperone??

Dame Dora *(nose to nose with the Sheriff)* Yes. I'm here to make sure there is no "hanky panky".

Sheriff Hanky panky?

Dame Dora Hanky panky.

Marian Stop saying hanky panky.
Dame Dora *(to the Sheriff)* What's that smell?

Sheriff It's my aftershave?

Dame Dora What's it called?

Sheriff Old Spice.

Dame Dora Old Spice? It smells more like Old Dead Mice.

Sheriff It's all the rage in Nottingham.

Dame Dora *(To the audience)* Do you know, a little bit of sick just came up in my throat.

Denchman the Henchman Lady Marian does not need a chaperone.

Dame Dora *(To Denchman)* I beg to differ. *(Flirty)* Tell me, handsome, are we having pre-dinner snacks?

Denchman the Henchman You are not staying for dinner, Dame Dora. The guards will show you out.

Dame Dora *(To Denchman)* You're very dominant, aren't you Denchman? I like that in a man.

Marian *(to the Sheriff)* If Dame Dora goes, I go.

Sheriff You will not say that when we are married, Maid Marian.

Marian *(in the Sheriff's face)* I will *never* marry you! *(To audience)* Oh, dear, that aftershave really is horrible. It's making my eyes water.

Sheriff You will learn to love me, Lady Marion. Or you will slowly perish in a prison cell.

Dame Dora You would not dare to say that if my son was here.

Sheriff Your son?
Dame Dora My son... Robin of Sherwood.

Sheriff Your son is Robin Hood?

Dame Dora Yes. And soon his Merry Men-Slash-Women will overthrow this castle and it will be *you* that is in a dungeon.

Sheriff Guards! Take her away!

Dame Dora *(pointing at Denchman)* I want *him* to throw me out.

Denchman the Henchman I'm busy.

Dame Dora *(to Denchman)* You're no fun.

Two castle guards grab hold of Dora and escort her from the stage.

Dame Dora Take your hands off me, you brutes. I am perfectly capable of throwing myself out.

The guards escort Dame Dora from the stage. The Sheriff takes Marian by the hand.

The pair walk forward and the tabs close behind them.

Song 5

They sing a duet in which the Sheriff declares his undying love and Marian rejects him.

Scene 3

Tabs open to reveal Sherwood Forest. The Merry Men/Women are onstage along with Long Face the Pantomime Horse.

Will Scarlett Hello Merry Men-Slash-Women!

Audience We're all very merry and we like cream and jelly!

Will Scarlett Welcome to Sherwood Forest where me and the rest of the Merry Men-Slash-Women live.

Little June The Sheriff and his men will never find us here.

Friar Tuck Even if they get a really good SatNav.

Will Scarlett *(To audience)* You already know Friar Tuck and Little June, and this is Long Face the horse.

Long Face *(Saying it flatly, without feeling)* Neigh.

Will Scarlett Long Face is a talking horse…

Long Face Neigh!

Will Scarlett But unfortunately he can only say one word.

Long Face Neigh.

Will Scarlett Which is "Neigh".

Long Face Neigh.

Will Scarlett Long Face, what's the opposite of "Aye"?

Long Face Neigh.

Will Scarlett Long Face, what's a word that rhymes with "play"?

Long Face Neigh.

Will Scarlett Long Face is highly intelligent, but he is a bit shy.

Long Face Neigh.

The sound of a horn.

Will Scarlett Heads up everyone, Robin's here.
Robin enters with Alan a Dale, a minstrel with a guitar strung across his back.

Robin Good news Merry Men-Slash-Women! We have a brand new member of our merry band. Alan a Dale.

Alan a Dale Hello everyone.

All Hello, Alan a Dale!

Long Face Neigh!

Will Scarlett Alan a Dale? That's an unusual name.

Friar Tuck Is that Alan, hyphen, a Dale?

Little June Or is it Alan, hyphen, "a", hyphen Dale.

Alan a Dale Neither. It's just plain old Alan a Dale.

Will Scarlett No hyphens?

Alan a Dale No hyphens.

Robin Does the "a" stand for something?

Friar Tuck Like a middle name. Arthur?

Alan a Dale No.

Will Scarlett Alexander?

Alan a Dale No.

Little June Alan?

Alan a Dale Alan?

Little June Yes.

Alan a Dale Alan's my first name. How could my middle name be the same as my first name?

Will Scarlett You could be Alan Alan.

Little June Yes. The second Alan could be spelt slightly differently from the first Alan. Maybe with a "u"?

Friar Tuck Or with two "L"s?

Alan a Dale No! I'm just plain, simple Alan a Dale. No hyphens. No middle name.

(Beat)

Robin Well, I'm glad we cleared that up.

Friar Tuck What do you do, Alan a Dale?

Alan a Dale I am a wandering minstrel.

Little June What's that?

Alan a Dale Well, I sing songs and sort of…. wander around.

Robin Can you sing songs *without* wandering around?

Alan a Dale What do you mean?

Robin Are you able to sing songs standing still?

Will Scarlett I don't know. I've never tried.

Robin Why don't you give it a try?

Alan a Dale Can't do any harm, I suppose.

Alan removes the guitar from his back and gets ready to strum it.

Alan a Dale A-one, a-two, a-one, two, three, four....

He makes a straining noise and tries to strum the guitar. But without success.

Alan a Dale It's no good. I can't sing unless I'm wandering around.

Robin Well, I think you should go for a little wander and sing a song for us.

Alan a Dale Alright, I will.

Robin Take it away, Alan!

Song 6

Alan a Dale walks forward. The tabs close behind him and he wanders around the front of the stage singing a song and playing his guitar.

Scene 4

Tabs open to reveal the village gymnasium. On the floor are set three steps for a step aerobics session. Enter Marian.

Marian Come on ladies! Hurry up! You don't want to be late for my first step aerobics class.

Dressed in brightly coloured gym gear, Dame Dora reluctantly trudges onto the stage, followed by Juliet.

Dame Dora What is "step aerobics"?

Marian Step aerobics is the very latest modern craze.

Dame Dora Modern craze? This is the twelfth century!

Juliet Don't you want to get fit?

Dame Dora I am fit.

Juliet *(under her breath)* Fit to burst.

Dame Dora *(To Juliet)* What was that?

Juliet Nothing.

Marion I am going to count to three, and I want you both to do what I do.

Dame Dora Right.

Marian One, two, three… step up.

They copy Marian and get onto their steps.

Dame Dora Ok, we've done that.

Juliet Now what?

Marian I'm going to count to three again and this time you get off your steps.

Dame Dora But we've only just got *onto* our steps.

Juliet What's the point of stepping onto our steps if we're immediately going to step off our steps again.

Marian Just do it.

Juliet This is stupid.

Marian One, two, three… step down.

They all get off their steps. Beat.

Dame Dora Well, that's my exercise for the day. I'm off to get a strawberry milkshake. Come on Juliet.

Juliet and Dame Dora start to exit.

Marian Where are you going?

Dame Dora That was very enjoyable, dear. Thanks for inviting us.

Marian But we haven't finished!

Juliet Haven't we?

Marian No! You have get up on your steps again!

Dame Dora Again?

Marian You've only done it once!!!

Dame Dora Well, how many times do we have to do it?

Marian I don't know, a thousand???

Dame Dora A thousand?

Marian Yes!!!

Dame Dora You want us to climb onto these steps, and back down again, a thousand times?

Juliet What's the point of that?

Marian It releases endorphins.

Dame Dora Dolphins?

Juliet Why would we want to release dolphins?

Marian Not dolphins!!

Dame Dora I'm confused.

Marian Dora, please! Just do as I say. Your buttocks will thank you for it.

Dame Dora My buttocks?

Marian Yes.

Dame Dora *(walking down to audience)* Ladies and gentlemen, in all my life - and it has been a very *long* life - I have heard many things. The sound of sweet birdsong in the morning, the heart-rending cry of a newborn baby, the gentle sound of a sea breeze wafting through the palm trees. But I have never, ever, heard the sound of my buttocks thanking me.

Marion Get back on your step!

Dame Dora In fact, as far as I'm aware, my buttocks have never said *anything* to me.

Marian Dora!!!

Dame Dora Yes, ma'am.

Dora runs back to her step. Marian starts stepping up and down again. Dora & Juliet copy her.

Marian *(faster)* One, two, three... up, one two, three... down.

Marian continues stepping, the others follow. Still stepping, Dame Dora gets out a pack of biscuits and stars crunching. Marian stops.

Marian *(To Dora)* What are you doing?

Dame Dora Eating biscuits.

Marian You can't eat biscuits while you're exercising!

Dame Dora Can't I?

Marian No!!!

Dame Dora *(To audience)* This activity will never catch on.

Dora puts the biscuits away.

Marian Right. One, two, three… up, one two, three… down.

Dame Dora and Juliet follow Marion's stepping again. They are struggling to keep up with the pace.

Dame Dora *(Stepping)* Marian… Can I ask you a question?

Marian *(Stepping)* Yes.

Dame Dora *(Stepping)* Under what circumstances am I allowed to stop doing this?

Marian *(Stepping)* You can only stop in the event of a medical emergency.

Dame Dora *(Stepping)* What about a clothing malfunction?

Marian *(Stepping)* What kind of clothing malfunction?

Dame Dora *(Stepping)* I think my bloomers are about to fall down.

Dora's bloomers fall to the floor. She pulls them up, and quickly runs off stage. Juliet and Marian stop stepping.

Marian Well, that didn't go very well, did it?

Juliet Not really.

Marian *(To Juliet)* Do you want to stop as well?

Juliet Well, I do want to look as fit as I can for….

Marian For who?

Juliet For Will, of course.

Marian Will Scarlett?

Juliet Yes. I think he's wonderful.

Marian Well, well. Imagine that. You and Will Scarlett.

Juliet Promise you won't tell anyone.

Marian I promise. On one condition.

Juliet What's that?

Marian That you promise to be my Maid of Honour when I marry Robin.

Juliet It's a deal.

Marion In the meantime, I think you'd better go and help Dame Dora sort out her clothing malfunction.

Juliet Good idea. See you later.

Exit Marion. Juliet walks to the front of the stage and the tabs close behind her.
Song 7

Juliet sings a romantic love song for Will Scarlett. Blackout.

Scene 5

Tabs open to reveal the Sheriffs Castle. Enter the Sheriff of Nottingham and Denchman the Henchman.

Sheriff *(to audience)* Ah ha! I see that you miserable bunch of smelly, scruffy peasants are still here...

Audience Boooo!

Sheriff I thought you would have crawled back to your nasty little hovels by now.

Audience Boooo!

Sheriff Denchman, where are you?

Denchman the Henchman runs on.

Denchman the Henchman You called, your grace?

Sheriff Yes Denchman. I have grave news. Lady Marian has once again spurned my advances...

Denchman the Henchman I'm sure she will live to regret it, your grace.

Sheriff What is worse, I hear that she loves that lanky, longbow-touting outlaw Robin Hood.

Denchman the Henchman Word on the street is that she plans to marry him.

Sheriff Marry him??? We cannot allow this, Denchman. We need to come up with a brilliant plan to get rid of Robin Hood for good.

Denchman the Henchman Hood for good?

Sheriff Hood for good. Do you have any brilliant ideas?

Denchman the Henchman Not as such.

Sheriff Denchman, I will count to three. And if you haven't come up with a brilliant plan by the end of that time I will send you to the dungeons and have my Chief Torturer poke you repeatedly with a very sharp object.

Denchman the Henchman I don't like very sharp objects.

Sheriff Of course you don't. I'm going to start counting now, Denchman.

Denchman the Henchman No!

Sheriff One...

Denchman the Henchman I'm too young to die.

Sheriff Two...

Denchman the Henchman I haven't even written a will.

Sheriff Three.

Denchman the Henchman Wait! I've got it!

Sheriff You have?

Denchman the Henchman Yes.

Sheriff Well, out with it, man!

Denchman the Henchman We start by laying a long trail of Liquorice Allsorts on the ground - starting from the edge of the forest where Robin Hood lives.

Sheriff I'm listening.

Denchman the Henchman Robin Hood will eat the Liquorice Allsorts, and the trail will slowly lead the outlaw to the inside of a big cardboard box, propped up with a stick.

Sheriff Go on....

Denchman the Henchman Then comes the best part. When he's underneath the box we tug on a long piece of string that's attached to the stick.

Sheriff The stick falls over, the box drops down, and Robin Hood is trapped inside.

Denchman the Henchman Yes.

(Long Pause)

Sheriff I like it.

Denchman the Henchman You do really?

Sheriff No, you idiot! It's the most stupid plan I've ever heard.

Denchman the Henchman Oh,

Sheriff In any case, I know for a fact that Robin Hood does not like Liquorice Allsorts

Denchman the Henchman Haribo?

Sheriff No.

Denchman the Henchman Hob Nobs?

Sheriff No. Do you have any other brilliant plans?

Denchman the Henchman Only one.

Sheriff What's that?

Denchman the Henchman Mystic Reg.

Sheriff Mystic Reg?

Denchman the Henchman Yes.

Sheriff Who is Mystic Reg?

Denchman the Henchman Mystic Reg is the most gifted, cunning sorcerer in all of Nottingham.

Sheriff Is he expensive?
Denchman the Henchman Yes. But I guarantee that Mystic Reg will come up with a way to get rid of Robin Hood.

Mystic Reg quickly runs on and stands behind the Sheriff.

Sheriff Very well. Bring Mystic Reg to me, with all haste.

Denchman the Henchman He's behind you.

Sheriff Don't be ridiculous. How can he be here already?

Denchman the Henchman Because, your grace, Mystic Reg is…. mystic.

Mystic Reg Good afternoon.

The Sheriff jumps in the air with surprise.

Sheriff Woh! *(Turning around)* You nearly gave me a heart attack.

Mystic Reg I have received a message, through the ether, that you wanted to see me.

Sheriff What's the ether?

Mystic Reg The ether is like the internet but more mysterious and magical.

Sheriff I see. Are you Mystic Reg?

Mystic Reg I am indeed Mystic Reg. Mystic by name, mystic by nature. *(sniffing)* I don't like your aftershave.

Denchman the Henchman Show some respect, man. You are in the presence of the Sheriff of Nottingham!

Mystic Reg Oh, I know who he is. I know everything about the Sheriff of Nottingham. *(To audience)* His birth sign is Aries, he enjoys fishing, playing table tennis and eating Cheesy Wotsits. His inside leg measurement is 34 inches, his hat size is 7, and he has a tattoo of Olly Murs on his left shoulder blade.
Sheriff Remarkable.

Mystic Reg *(To Sheriff)* Your grace, I have already read your mind and I know your every whim, your every desire and your every ambition. I also know why you have called me here.

Sheriff Go on…

Mystic Reg You want to know… next week's National Lottery numbers.

Sheriff Wrong.

Mystic Reg But it's a rollover week.

Sheriff I want you to help me to get rid of Robin Hood.

Mystic Reg Robin Hood?

Sheriff Yes.

Mystic Reg But Robin Hood robs from the rich and gives to the poor.

Sheriff I know.

Mystic Reg Which is an excellent business model.

Sheriff Supposedly.

Mystic Reg The people of Nottingham love him!

Denchman the Henchman We are quite aware of that.

Mystic Reg Oh, I get it.

Sheriff What?

Mystic Reg This is about Maid Marian isn't it?

Denchman the Henchman How do you know that?
Mystic Reg Maid Marian is the most beautiful woman in Nottingham. She's bound to have a thing for a wild, reckless, handsome outlaw like Robin Hood.

Sheriff Am I not handsome?

Mystic Reg In your dreams.

Sheriff Well? Can you help me get rid me of the outlaw formally known as Prince of Thieves?

Mystic Reg hands a little piece of paper to the Sheriff.

Mystic Reg Here are my bank details. Deposit 500 groats in my account and we can get started.

Sheriff 500 groats? That's way too much.

Mystic Reg What if I let you have a 20% discount for being a new customer.

Sheriff Done.

Mystic Reg And you have been.

Sheriff What's the plan?

Mystic Reg We will hold an archery contest.

Sheriff An archery contest?

Mystic Reg With a big cash prize for the winner. Once Robin Hood hears about that there is no way he will be able to resist coming to the castle. And once you've got him here you can arrest him!

Sheriff It's devilish! It's despicable! Denchman, what's another word for "despicable" that starts with a "d"?

Denchman the Henchman Diabolical?
Sheriff Perfect. Deliciously diabolical. But wait! They say that Robin Hood is the best archer in all of Nottingham. What if he *wins* the archery contest?

Mystic Reg Then you simply go to VAR and disallow it.

Sheriff Brilliant! Mystic Reg, I can see that you are going to become an extremely valuable member of my team.

Song 8

The Sheriff, Denchman and Mystic Reg walk forward and the tabs close behind them. They sing a song about being bad. At the end of the song, blackout.

Scene 6

Tabs open on the forest. On stage are all of Robin's Merry Men/Women and Long Face the Pantomime Horse

Will Scarlett *(To audience)* Hello Merry Men-Slash-Women!

Audience We're all very merry and we like cream and jelly!

Will Scarlett Listen up everyone! The Sheriff of Nottingham has announced a contest to find the finest archer in the land.

Friar Tuck Well, we all know that's Robin!

Alan a Dale He's probably be best archer in the world!

Little June The best archer in the universe!

Robin Steady on, chaps.

Will Scarlett The winner will be presented with a thousand groats, and a solid gold bow and arrow.

Friar Tuck Hold on, how do we know that it's not a trap?
Robin A trap?

Friar Tuck A trap to lure Robin into the Sheriff's castle.

Little June It does sound a little too good to be true.

Will Scarlett Do you think it's a trap, Long Face?

Long Face Neigh.

Friar Tuck Was that a yes or a no?

Will Scarlett I don't know. *(To the horse)* Long Face, tap your hoof twice for yes and once for no. Do you think Robin is being led into a trap?

Long Face taps his hoof twice.

Will Scarlett Was that a yes.

Long Face Neigh!

Will Scarlett *(To audience)* This is clearly going nowhere.

Alan a Dale Well, I don't think you should risk it, Robin.

Robin Never fear, Merry Men-Slash-Women. I shall go to the contest… in disguise!

Friar Tuck Disguise?

Robin In fact, we shall *all* go to the castle in disguise?

All Hoorah!

Song 9

Robin and the Merry Men/Women walk downstage and the tabs close behind them. They sing a rousing song together.

Scene 7

Tabs open on the Castle Courtyard. The stage is set for an archery contest. There are several castle guards and a few villagers waiting for the contest to start. The Sheriff enters with Denchman the Henchman.

The Sheriff At last, the day of the archery contest! *(To audience)* I hope all you filthy, moth-eaten peasants are looking forward to seeing Robin Hood arrested and thrown into the castle dungeons.

Audience Boooooo!

The Sheriff Oh, shut up.

Denchman the Henchman Everything is made ready, your grace.

The Sheriff produces a list, and ticks it off with a long feathered quill pen.

The Sheriff Checklist. Have you erected the target?

Denchman the Henchman Yes.

The Sheriff Have you mixed water with the wine in the wine barrels?

Denchman the Henchman Yes.

The Sheriff Have you fixed it so that I win all the raffle prizes?

Denchman the Henchman Yes.

The Sheriff Have you set up that fairground stall where you can win a goldfish by throwing hoops over boxes.

Denchman the Henchman Yes.

The Sheriff Have you made sure that the boxes are slightly bigger than the hoops so that the hoops don't fit over the boxes?

Denchman the Henchman Yes.
The Sheriff Good! And don't forget, I am relying on *you* to win the archery contest!

Denchman the Henchman Me?

The Sheriff You can shoot a bow and arrow can't you?

Denchman the Henchman Well, yes, but…

The Sheriff No buts, Denchman. If you do not beat Robin Hood to the big prize you will end this day with your head on a spike.

Denchman the Henchman A spike?

The Sheriff The pointiest, tallest spike in all of Nottingham.

Denchman the Henchman Gulp.

The Sheriff What's that?

Denchman the Henchman I said "gulp", your grace.

Enter Dame Dora, Maid Marian and Juliet.

Juliet *(To Marian)* So, Marian, do you think the Sheriff will ask you to marry him today?

Dame Dora If he does, I'll give him a piece of my mind.

Maid Marian Are you sure you can spare it, Dora?

Dame Dora Don't be cheeky.

Juliet I've heard a rumor that Robin is coming here today. To try and win the archery contest.

Dame Dora But what if it's a trap to catch him?

Maid Marian Don't worry. The Sheriff isn't bright enough to outwit Robin. He's only just worked out how to put on his own socks.

Denchman the Henchman approaches them.

Denchman the Henchman Lady Marian, the Sheriff requests that you sit next to him during the archery contest.

Maid Marian Do I have to?

Juliet You'd better go, Marian.

Dame Dora *(to Denchman)* And can I sit next to you, cheeky boy?

Denchman the Henchman *(To Dame Dora)* Absolutely not.

Dame Dora Spoilsport.

Denchman the Henchman *(To Marian)* Follow me, Lady Marian.

Dame Dora Keep your hand on your holiday money, Marian!

Marian goes and sits next to the Sheriff. Dame Dora and Juliet join the crowd of villagers.

Enter Will Scarlett, Alan a Dale, Friar Tuck, Little June and Long Face the Horse. They are all wearing some sort of disguise. Various ridiculous hats, dark glasses, moustaches and beards. Long Face is wearing a big pair of horns on his head and has a large pink udder strung underneath his girth. The men whisper loudly to each other.

Friar Tuck Are you sure the Sheriff's men are not going to recognise us?

Will Scarlett Absolutely not. These disguises are completely foolproof. Just mingle with the villagers and wait for Robin to arrive.

Little June What's Long Face the Pantomime Horse come as?

Friar Tuck He's come as a pantomime cow.

Will Scarlett *(To the audience)* A pantomime horse disguised as a pantomime cow. You won't see that at the Palladium.

Robin enters dressed as a big rabbit. Even though his face is clearly visible through a hole in the front of the costume, no-one recognises him.

Friar Tuck Where's is Robin?

Alan a Dale I haven't seen him.

Will Scarlett Well, he was supposed to be here by now.

Little June Go and ask that big rabbit if he's seen him.

Will Scarlett Good idea.

Will Scarlett walks over to the rabbit and whispers to him.

Will Scarlett Excuse me…

Robin *(in rabbit costume)* Yes?

Will Scarlett Have you seen our friend Robin Hood, anywhere?

Robin What does he look like?

Will Scarlett It's hard to say. He's in disguise.

Robin Well, how tall is he?

Will Scarlett About the same height as you.

Robin I'll look out for him.

Will Scarlett Thank you.

Will Scarlett walks back to where the other Merry Men/Women are standing.

Little June What did the big rabbit say?

Will Scarlett He said he'd keep his eyes peeled for Robin.

Alan a Dale *(Sudden realisation)* Wait a minute…

Will Scarlett What?

Alan a Dale How can that rabbit look out for Robin if he doesn't know what disguise he's wearing?

Will Scarlett I didn't think of that.

The rabbit shuffles over to the Merry Men/Women and stands behind them.

Robin Pssssssst!

Friar Tuck What was that noise?

Little June What noise?

Alan a Dale It was a noise like this: "Pssssssst!"

Will Scarlett What makes a noise like "Pssssssst"?

Friar Tuck I don't know. A rabbit?

Robin Pssssssst!

Friar Tuck There it is again.

Robin lifts up the small rabbit's nose he's been wearing on his face.

Robin It's me.

Everyone turns around to look at Robin.

Little June Robin?
Robin Yes!

Will Scarlett What a brilliant disguise!

Robin Thank you.

Friar Tuck No-one will *ever* guess that the big rabbit in the archery contest is Robin Hood.

Will Scarlett Long Face, did you guess that the big rabbit was Robin?

Long Face Moo.

Little June I thought he could only say "neigh."

Will Scarlett He's in disguise.

The Sheriff rises from his seat and address the crowd.

Sheriff Ladies and Gentlemen, boys and girls. The grand archery contest is about to begin. The archer whose arrow is closest to the centre of the target will be crowned champion of all Nottingham and win the cash prize of a thousand groats.

Alan a Dale *(Whisper)* Exactly how much is a groat?

Friar Tuck *(Whisper)* About four pence.

Alan a Dale *(Whisper)* Is that all?

Friar Tuck *(Whisper)* That's enough to buy a four bedroom house in the twelfth century.

Alan a Dale *(Whisper)* How do you know?

Friar Tuck *(Whisper)* I saw it on Location, Location, Location.

Sheriff Let the contest begin! Will the first archer please step up to the oche.
A villager appears from the crowd and stands before the target.

Sheriff The very best of order, please.

The villager fires his arrow. It misses the target and goes into the wings. A moment later a dead bird with an arrow through it is chucked onto the stage.

Sheriff Next!

A second villager steps forward. He also misses the target and his arrow flies off into the wings. A moment later one of the castle guards staggers onstage with an arrow sticking out of his chest. He spins around dramatically a few times, emits a loud cough, and collapses onto the floor. Two other guards quickly drag him off.

Will Scarlett *(To audience)* Well, he was clearly after a BAFTA.

Sheriff Are there any other contestants?

Villagers No!

Sheriff Is that strange-looking cow in the competition?

Will Scarlett Nope.

Sheriff Then I shall now introduce the finest archer in Nottingham. Please welcome Denchman the Henchman.

There is a ripple of applause. Denchman steps up to the oche. After carefully taking aim he fires his arrow straight into the center of the target.*

*Note: This effect is usually achieved either by having spring-loaded flip-out arrows on the front of the target, or by quickly pushing arrows through

the target from the rear. Alternatively the whole scene can be mimed using no arrows at all.

The crowd cheers.

Sheriff Excellent shooting Denchman! Bullseye! Ladies and gentlemen it appears that we have a winner!

Robin *(as big rabbit)* Wait! I believe that I can do better than that!

Sheriff Don't be ridiculous. How could a big rabbit get closer to the bullseye than that? Denchman's arrow is right in the centre.

Robin I can see that, your grace. But I still say I can get closer.

First Villager Let the rabbit shoot!

Second Villager Yes, give the big bunny a chance!

All *(chanting)* Let the rabbit shoot! Let the rabbit shoot! Let the rabbit shoot!

Sheriff Silence, you rabble! Very well. The rabbit can have a shot.

All Hooray!

Robin slowly takes aim at the target.. The crowd gasp. He fires his arrow and it splits Denchman the Henchman's arrow clean in two.

All Hooray!

Denchman carefully studies the target

Denchman the Henchman He's split my arrow clean in two!

The Sheriff and Will Scarlett go and examines the arrows in the target.
Sheriff How on earth did he do that?

Will takes a quick peep behind the target and tries to conceal a smile.

Will Scarlett I think we'd all like to know that.

Sheriff *(Clapping slowly)* Ladies and gentlemen, this was quite clearly an extraordinary shot. A one in an million shot! I therefore declare that this nig rabbit is the finest archer in the land!

Villagers Hooray!

Sheriff But wait. There is only one man in Nottingham who could have pulled off that shot. Denchman, unmask that rabbit!

Denchman the Henchman yanks the rabbit hood and big ears from Robin's head.

Maid Marian Robin?

Sheriff Just as I suspected! Robin Hood!

Robin Good afternoon everyone.

Sheriff Guards! Seize that rabbit – I mean seize that man! - and throw him into the castle dungeons.

Maid Marian No! Take your hands off him!

Robin *(To the audience)* Don't worry everyone. During the interval I'll figure out a brilliant way of escaping. *(Posing)* For I am Robin Hood!

The guards drag Robin away.

Song 10

The villagers, guards and disguised Merry Men/Women sing a big finale song for the end of Act 1. At the end of the song the Sheriff puts his arm around Maid Marion and leads her off. The Merry Men/Women run away.

Curtain.

END OF ACT ONE

ACT TWO

Scene 1

Tabs open on Sherwood Forest.

Song 11

Marion, Juliet and the Merry Men/Women all sing a rousing, optimistic song. Long Face the Horse does a little dance. At the end of the song, Will Scarlett steps forward.

Will Scarlett "Hello Merry Men-Slash-Women!"

Audience We're all very merry and we like cream and jelly!

Will Scarlett Welcome back to Sherwood Forest. Did you have a good interval?

Audience Yes!

Will Scarlett It's great to see you all. But I'm afraid the Merry Men-Slash-Women are not quite as merry as usual. Because our boss Robin Hood is still being held prisoner in the Sheriff of Nottingham's castle. What we need is an ingenious plan to rescue Robin. Anyone?

The Merry Men/Women all look at each other blankly.

Will Scarlett *(To the horse)* Long Face, do you have a plan?

Long Face Neigh.

Marian As long as King Richard is out of the country the Sheriff will continue to wreak havoc on the people of Nottingham and Sherwood.

Friar Tuck Then, we need to find the king and bring him back to the kingdom.

Alan a Dale If Richard knew what was happening to his people, he'd return home straight away, arrest the Sheriff and set Robin free.

Will Scarlett Does anyone know where the king is?

Little June Last I heard he was in Spain.

Will Scarlett Leading an army?

Little June No. I think he's playing golf.

Will Scarlett Then one of us must go and fetch him right away. There's no time to lose.

Alan a Dale I'll go. There's nothing a wandering minstrel likes better than a bloomin' good wander.

Will Scarlett Why don't you take Long Face the Horse?

Long Face Neigh.

Alan a Dale If you think I'm climbing onto the back of that thing, you've got another think coming.

Will Scarlett Boys and girls, do you think Alan should climb onto the back of Long Face the Horse?

Audience Yes!

The horse nods "no".

Alan a Dale Oh, all right then. Come on Long Face…

Alan a Dale has three clumsy attempts to climb onto the back of the panto horse. He finally manages it after taking a short run up. It's not a pretty sight.

Will Scarlett *(To the rear end of the horse)* Are you all right in there?

Long Face *(Muffled voice from rear end)* Yes.

All Hoorah!

Alan a Dale Wish me luck, everyone!

All Good luck, Alan a Dale! Good luck Long Face!

Alan gracelessly rides off stage, clinging perilously to the back end of the horse.

Friar Tuck *(To audience)* That was awkward.

Will Scarlett *(To Juliet)* There goes a very brave man.

Juliet Well, I think you're very brave as well, Will Scarlett.

Will Scarlett Really?

Juliet Yes. You're every bit as clever and charismatic as Robin Hood.

Will Scarlett Wow! Thank you.

She takes him by the hand.

Juliet I'm so happy I met you, Will Scarlett.

Will Scarlett I'm happy I met you too, Juliet.

Song 12

Will Scarlett and Juliet sing a chirpy, happy song together.

Scene 2

Tabs open on the Castle Dungeons. Robin is behind bars. Dame Dora enters carrying a tray of food for Robin.

Dame Dora Here you are, Robin, I've brought you some food.

Robin Thanks, mother. What is it?

Dame Dora It's a cheese and Marmite sandwich.

Robin Aw! My favourite. *(Takes a bite)* Let's hope it doesn't turn out to be my last supper.

Dame Dora Robin, I have good news and I have bad news. Which would you like first?

Robin The bad news?

Dame Dora The Sheriff has told Marian that if she doesn't marry him he will get rid of you for good.

Robin Well, I'd rather die than see the Sheriff married to Marian. What's the good news?

Dame Dora Marian is coming to visit you. In fact here she is now.

Marian enters.

Maid Marian Oh, Robin!

Robin Marian!

Dame Dora I'll wait outside. I'm sure one of the prison guards has taken a fancy to me.

Dame Dora exits.

Robin and Marian embrace through the prison bars.

Robin It's so good to see you, Marian.

Marian I simply had to come and visit. *(Sniffs)* Have you been eating Marmite?

Robin Yes.

Marian Weird.

Robin You shouldn't have come here, Marian. It's far too risky.

Marian I'd risk anything to be with you, Robin.

Song 13

*Robin and Marion sing a slow, romantic love due together.
At the end of the song...*

Robin Mother told me about the Sheriff's offer. Marian, you simply *can't* marry him! I'll work out a way to escape from here and then we can be together forever.

Marian But, I've already said yes, Robin. It's the only way to save your life.

Robin No!

Marian The wedding's tomorrow.

Robin Tomorrow?

Marian Yes. The Sheriff has already ordered the wedding cake.

Robin Please tell me that my mother is not making the wedding cake.

Marian No.

Robin Thank goodness for that.

Marian She's making the jellies.

Robin Seriously?

Marian The Sheriff says she must make the jellies for the wedding or he will banish her from the kingdom.

Robin Bit harsh.

Marian And he'll take away her bus pass.

Robin Oh dear.

Robin Who *is* making the wedding cake?

Marian Paul Hollywood.

Robin Figures.

Enter Dame Dora.

Dame Dora Marian you have to go. The guards are starting to get suspicious.

Marian *(To Dame Dora)* I'm coming, Dora. *(To Robin)* I love you, Robin!

Robin I love you too. And don't worry, everything will turn out fine!

Marian runs off. Blackout. Curtain.

Scene 3

Enter Dame Dora and Will Scarlett on tabs.

Will Scarlett *(Sadly)* "Hello Merry Men-Slash-Women!"

Audience "We're all very merry and we like cream and jelly!"

Will Scarlett News update. Robin's still locked up in the Sheriff's castle and there's still no word yet from Alan a Dale and Long Face who have gone to track down King Richard.

Dame Dora Cheer up Will. Things do have a habit of turning out for the best in pantomimes.

Will Scarlett I hope so. What shall we do to cheer ourselves up?

Dame Dora Well, we could try thinking about our favourite things.

Will Scarlett No! I hate that song!

Dame Dora What about writing a long list of reasons to be cheerful.

Will Scarlett I don't like that song either.

Dame Dora We could play a game.

Will Scarlett What game?

Dame Dora I'll think of something and you have to guess what it is.

Will Scarlet I love that game.

Dame Dora I can only answer yes or no.

Will Scarlett Right.

Dame Dora Ready?

Will Scarlett Yes.

Dame Dora Ok, I'm thinking about something.

Will thinks hard for a moment.

Will Scarlett Is it a chicken?

Dame Dora Yes! How on earth did you know I was thinking about a chicken?

Will Scarlett I don't know. Lucky guess I suppose? Start again.

Dame Dora OK, I'm thinking of something.

Will Scarlett Is it another chicken?

Dame Dora Yes!

Will Scarlett Why did you think of another chicken?

Dame Dora I thought it would throw you off the scent.

Will Scarlett Start again. Are you thinking of something?

Dame Dora Yes.

(Beat)

Will Scarlett Chicken?

Dame Dora Oh, for heaven's sake.

Will Scarlett Why don't you think about something else?

Dame Dora I like chickens.

Will Scarlett This is a stupid game. It's just you thinking about chickens, and me telling you that you're thinking about chickens. Can we play a different game?

Dame Dora We haven't got time. I need to finish making the jellies for the Sheriff's wedding. Will you help me?

Will Scarlett Are there any chickens involved?

Dame Dora No chickens.

Will Scarlett *(Calling out)* Have they finished changing the scenery?

Backstage voice Yes!

Will Scarlett *(To the audience)* That's quicker than last night.

Dame Dora Come on, let's go.
Will Scarlett I'm right behind you, Dora.

Tabs open to reveal "Dame Dora's Artisan Bakery". Will and Dora walk onto the set. There is a long table with many paper plates of jelly on it, and a big tube of squirty cream. There is plastic sheeting on the stage around the table.

Will Scarlett Crikey! That is a *lot* of jelly.

Dane Dora That's because everyone in Sherwood is very merry and likes cream and jelly.

Will Scarlett *(winking to audience)* I have heard that. So, how does this work?

Dame Dora We're going to walk along that long line of jellies.

Will Scarlett Yes…

Dame Dora You hold up each jelly in front of me, and I'll put a squirt of cream on top of it

Will Scarlett What could possibly go wrong?

Dame Dora Nothing. It's quite simple.

Will Scarlett Right.

While Dame Dora isn't looking, Will slyly picks up the squirty cream and sprays some into his mouth.

Dame Dora I saw that.

Will Scarlett Saw what?

Dame Dora You had some squirty cream.

Will Scarlett No I didn't.

Dame Dora You did. *(To audience)* Boys and girls, did Will have some squirty cream?

Audience Yes!

Will Scarlett Oh, no I didn't!

Audience Oh ,yes you did!

Will Scarlett Oh, no I didn't!

Audience Oh, yes you did!

Ad lib with audience.

Dame Dora Enough of this audience participation! Hold up the jellies, Will.

Will Scarlett Right.

One after another, Will holds up the first three jellies. Dame Dora quickly puts a squirt of cream on each of them.

Will Scarlett One jelly… two jellies… three jellies…

Will Scarlett pushes the third jelly into Dame Dora's face.

Dame Dora What did you do that for???

Will Scarlett Sorry. I couldn't resist it.

Dame Dora Why not?

Will Scarlett It's a panto.

Dame Dora That's no excuse!

Will Scarlett And they have put plastic sheeting down on the stage.

Dame Dora Behave yourself.

Will Scarlett Shame to waste it.

Dame Dora This time *I* will hold up the jellies.

Will Scarlett Ok.

Dame Dora And *you* will squirt the cream.

Dora hands Will the squirty cream. He immediately squirts some into his mouth.

Dame Dora Will you stop doing that!!!

Will Scarlett Sorry.

Dame Dora Are you ready?

Will Scarlett Yes.

One after another, Dame Dora holds up the next three jellies. Will quickly puts a squirt of cream on each of them.

Dame Dora One jelly… two jellies… three jellies…

On the third jelly, Will Scarlett pushes Dame Dora's hand into her own face, covering it in jelly and cream.

Dame Dora You did it again!!!

Will Scarlett I can't help it! It's too tempting.

Dame Dora Right, this time I'm not going to hold up the jellies. We'll leave them on the table.

Will Scarlett Good idea.

Dame Dora Then you won't be tempted.
Will Scarlett No.

Will very quickly squirts some cream into his mouth again.

Dame Dora I saw that ugly move.

Will squirts cream onto the next three jellies on the table.

Will Scarlett One jelly… two jellies… three jellies.

Dame Dora You did it! Well done.

Will Scarlett Thank you.

Will picks up two plates of jelly and cream and pushes them both into Dame Dora's face at the same time.

Dame Dora I suppose you think that's funny.

Will Scarlett Let's ask the audience. *(To audience)* Was that funny, boys and girls?

Audience Yes!!!

Dame Dora Ok, you've had your fun. We've really got to get this finished now.

Will Scarlett Yes.

Dame Dora No more jellies in the face?

Will Scarlett No more jellies in the face.

Dame Dora You stand there.

Will Scarlett Here?

Dame Dora Yes, there. Don't move.

Will Scarlett I won't move.

Dame Dora I'm going to go along the line and put cream onto some more of the jellies.

Will Scarlett Ok.

Dame Dora You count.

Will Scarlett I'll count.

Dame Dora goes along the line and puts cream onto another six jellies.

Will Scarlett One jelly... two jellies... three jellies... four jellies, five jellies, six jellies.

Dame Dora Well, at least you can count up to six.

Will Scarlett *(To audience)* This is like Sesame Street.

Dame Dora Now, Will Scarlett, come over here.

Will goes and stands close to the six newly cream-covered jellies.

Will Scarlett Here?

Dame Dora A little to your left.

Will Scarlett Here?

Dame Dora Perfect.

Will Scarlett Now what?

Dame Dora picks up a plate of jelly and cream

Dame Dora What should I do, boys and girls?

Audience reaction. Dora holds one plate of jelly and cream very close to Will's face?

Dame Dora Should I do it, boys and girls?

Audience Yes!!!

Dame Dora Should I?

Audience Yes!!!

Will quickly grabs the plate from Dame Dora and shoves the jelly and cream into her face.

Dame Dora That does it!

Will and Dora throw several plates of jelly at each other. It is chaos. Finally, peace breaks out. Pause.

Will Scarlett One for luck?

Dame Dora squirts cream onto one last jelly and shoves it into Will's face.

Will Scarlett Thank you.

Dame Dora You're welcome.

Will Scarlett Mmm, strawberry flavour.

Dame Dora I think we'd better clean up this mess!

Will Scarlett What are you going to give the wedding guests now?

Dame Dora I don't know. I'll think of something.

Curtain.

Scene 4

Enter Friar Tuck & Little June on tabs.

Little June What are you reading Friar Tuck?

Friar Tuck It's an official parchment from the castle. I am ordered to marry the Sheriff.

Little June I thought Marian was marrying the Sheriff.

Friar Tuck No, not marry the Sheriff. *Marry* the Sheriff.

Little June Oh, of course! You're a Friar!

Friar Tuck Well spotted!

Little June So you can perform a wedding ceremony.

Friar Tuck Fully qualified.

Little June But you can't preside over a wedding where the bride wants to marry someone else!

Friar Tuck What choice do I have?

Little June How about reading the marriage service with your fingers crossed behind your back.

Friar Tuck What?

Little June That would mean you don't actually *mean* anything you say.

Friar Tuck I don't think English Law works like that, Little June.

Little June You could pretend to faint?

Friar Tuck Faint? But I'm a *terrible* actor.

Little June We've noticed.

Friar Tuck What?

Little June Nothing. I've got an idea.

Friar Tuck What?

Little June You could hide a broadsword underneath your habit, and half way through the service you could draw the sword and challenge the Sheriff to a duel.

Friar Tuck I can't use a broadsword.

Little June How about a slightly less broad sword?

Friar Tuck No.

Little June A really narrow sword?

Friar Tuck No.

Little June A tiny, tiny sword?

Friar Tuck I am not able to use a sword of any size.

Little June Oh dear. Can you fire a longbow?

Friar Tuck No.

Little June A medium bow?

Friar Tuck No.

Little June A short bow?

Friar Tuck I can't shoot a bow of *any* size!

Little June Oh. Well, if you can't use a bow and arrow or a sword, how did you get into Robin's Merry Men-Slash-Women?

Friar Tuck Because, Little June…

Little June Go on…

Friar Tuck Promise you won't laugh.

Little June I won't laugh.

Friar Tuck It was because I can do this.

Pumping dance music kicks in. Friar Tuck performs a short but impressive hip-hop dance routine. Audience probably applaud. Beat.

Little June Do that again.

Friar Tuck does the little routine again.

Little June *(To audience)* You never really know a person, do you?

Friar Tuck Come on Little June, we'd better get back to the camp.

Exit Little June and Friar Tuck, music pumping. Tabs open to reveal the forest. It is very dark and shadowy and there is an eerie mist drifting across the stage.

Will Scarlett Hello, Merry Men-Slash-Women!

Audience We're all very merry and we love cream and jelly!

Dame Dora I've walked from the bakery to the castle hundreds of times, but I just can't get my bearings in this fog. I've got a horrible feeling that we're lost.

Will Scarlett All the trees look the same in the mist.

Dame Dora And it's getting dark fast. The wild animals will be out and about soon.

Juliet Don't worry, Dame Dora. My Will is here to protect us.

Will Scarlett I'll do my best, Juliet. But I'll need some help. *(To audience)* Will you warn me if you see anything strange in the forest, boys and girls?

Audience Yes!

Will Scarlett After dark, this can be a very scary and creepy place…

While Will is talking to the audience, one of the trees upstage moves from one side of the set to the other. The audience react.

Will Scarlett Did you see something, boys and girls?

Audience Yes!

Will Scarlett Where was it?

Audience Behind you!

Will Scarlett What's that? Was it behind me?

Audience Yes!

Will and the others turn around. The tree is now stationary.

Dame Dora I think you must be imagining things, boys and girls. There's nothing there.

They all turn back to face the audience. The tree waddles across stage again. Audience react.

Juliet What is it? Can you see something? Where is it?

Audience Behind you! /The tree moved!

Will Scarlett They're saying that one of those trees moved.

Dame Dora Don't be ridiculous, Will Scarlett. Trees don't move. *(To audience)* Did a tree move, boys and girls?

Audience Yes!

Juliet Where did you see it?

Audience Behind you!

The tree once again moves from one side of the stage to the other.

Audience react.

Dame Dora *(audience)* I don't know what everyone shouting about.

Juliet Can you see something boys and girls?

Audience Behind you!

The tree once again moves from one side of the stage to the other. This time Will Scarlett turns around just in time to see it.

Will Scarlett The tree *did* move. But you don't have to worry, boys and girls. This tree is a friend of mine.

Juliet A friend?

Will Scarlett Yes. This is my good friend Leafworm. He's one of the friendly tree spirits of Sherwood Forest.

Dame Dora *(To audience)* Tree spirits? Now I've seen everything.

Will Scarlett Come and say hello to the boys and girls, Leafworm.

The tree waddles downstage. There is a hole cut in the trunk so that we can see its face.

Leafworm Hello boys and girls.

Will Scarlett How are you Leafworm? I haven't seen you for a while.

Leafworm I've been on display in a garden at the Chelsea Flower Show.

Will Scarlett Really?

Leafworm Yes. Monty Don gave me a silver gilt medal.

Will Scarlett In what category?

Leafworm Best talking tree.

Will Scarlett Congratulations.

Leafworm Thank you. But I'm here to warn you. There are some very mischievous ghosts at large in the forest tonight.

Will Scarlett Oh dear.

Juliet Ghosts???

Leafworm You should get to the castle as quickly as you can. I will lead the way.

Dame Dora What a load of old nonsense. I, for one, do not believe in ghosts. *(aside to audience)* Talking trees, yes, ghosts no.

Will Scarlett *(To audience)* You will warn us if you see any ghosts, won't you boys and girls.

Audience Yes!!!

Leafworm Follow me, everyone.

Dame Dora, Juliet and Will Scarlett slowly follow Leafworm. Meanwhile, upstage, three very scary ghosts move one by one through the forest. Audience react.
Audience Behind you!

All Aggghhhhh!!! Ghosts!

The ghosts chase Dame Dora, Juliet, Will Scarlett and Leafworm round and around in circles.

Ghosts Wooooooooh!

Dame Dora Run away! Run away!

Ghosts Wooooooooh!

All Run away!

Finally, Dame Dora holds up her hand for everyone to stop.

Dame Dora Woh! Everyone, stop! Hold it right there!

They all skid to a halt.

Dame Dora Now, we can all run round and around in circles all night. Or, we can sort this out. Which of you ghosts is the leader?

One of the ghosts sheepishly puts up their hand.

Dame Dora You! What exactly is it that you want from us?

The ghost waves its arms around and howls.

Dame Dora *(To Leafworm)* What did it say?

Leafworm The ghost says they will let us pass peacefully on our way.

Juliet That's a relief.

Leafworm But only on one condition.

Will Scarlett What's that?
Leafworm They want to do a song.

Dame Dora *(To the ghosts)* Well, why didn't you say so before?

Song 14

Dame Dora, Juliet, Will Scarlett and Leafworm sing a scary song with the ghosts. At the end of the song the ghosts all disappear and Leafworm blends back into the background with the other trees. The lights slowly come up.

Juliet The ghosts have gone.

Dame Dora Thank goodness for that.

Will Scarlett I rather liked them.

Juliet It's getting light. I can see the castle ahead.

Dame Dora That's a relief.

Long Face *(offstage)* Neigh!

Will Scarlett Wait! That sounded like Long Face the Pantomime Horse.

Long Face *(offstage)* Neigh!

Dame Dora It *is* Long Face!

Enter Alan a Dale and Long Face.

Will Scarlett And here's Alan a Dale!

Dame Dora You're back safely! But where is King Richard?

Enter King Richard carrying a bag of golf clubs.

King Richard My loyal subjects!

They all fall to their knees.
Dame Dora Your majesty!

King Richard It's good to be back in England. But, there is no need for ceremony. You can all get up now.

Dame Dora *(To audience)* That's easier said than done.

Will Scarlett helps Dame Dora to her feet.

Dame Dora Oooh, me coccyx.

King Richard Alan a Dale has told me much of the wicked doings of the Sheriff of Nottingham.

Dame Dora What shall we do?

King Richard We shall go right away to the Sheriff's castle and release Robin of Sherwood.

All Hooray!

Juliet And then Robin can marry Marion.

All Hooray!

Will Scarlett But the castle is protected by hundreds of guards. How will we get past them?

King Richard The guards will not dare betray their king. As soon as they see my face they will lay down their arms. Then, the Sheriff of Nottingham's dreadful reign of terror will be over.

Will Scarlett To the castle!

They all run off. Curtain.

Song 15

Enter Marian on tabs. She is wearing a wedding dress and sings a sad and poignant love song to Robin.

Scene 5

Tabs open on the Castle Courtyard. It is set for a wedding. Castle guards and villagers wait for the ceremony to begin.

Some of the villagers are wearing big capes and hoods that cover their faces.

The Sheriff enters with Denchman the Henchman.

Sheriff *(To audience)* My wedding day at last! A day that will make me the happiest man in the kingdom and Maid Marion the most miserable girl in the world!

Audience Boooooo!

Sheriff *(To audience)* Oh, be quiet. You're lucky to be invited to a wedding.

Denchman the Henchman Everything is prepared, your grace.

Sheriff Did you buy plenty of confetti for the peasants to throw?

Denchman the Henchman I'm sorry, the castle rules do not allow confetti to be thrown at weddings.

Sheriff No confetti? But it's *my* castle!

Denchman the Henchman No exceptions I'm afraid.

Sheriff Curses. What about the jellies and cream?

Denchman the Henchman I'm afraid there was also an issue with those, your grace.

Sheriff An issue???

Denchman the Henchman Yes, but the bakery has sent a substitute item.

Sheriff What is it?

Denchman the Henchman Jaffa Cakes.

Sheriff Jaffa Cakes??? I can't give my wedding guests Jaffa Cakes!!! *(To audience)* Sigh! Sometimes it's not easy being an evil tyrant.

Denchman the Henchman I quite like Jaffa Cakes.

Sheriff Don't just stand there, Denchman. Let's get this wedding started!

Denchman the Henchman Guards! Fetch the bride!

The Sheriff takes his place at the alter with Denchman the Henchman alongside him as best man.

Maid Marion is led onstage by two guards and positioned next to the Sheriff. Friar Tuck enters and stands before them. Mystic Reg also enters and stands nearby as a witness.

Sheriff Marian... how beautiful you look.

Marian I wish I could same the same for you.

Friar Tuck Dearly beloved, we are gathered here today in the eyes of the Lord, to join together this man...

Sheriff Do you mind if we speed this up a bit? I want to get to the nibbles before they all get eaten.

Friar Tuck Very well. Do you Robert de Bentley de Renault de Volvo, High Sheriff of Nottingham, take this lady to be your lawfully wedded wife?

Sheriff Yes, I do! Absolutely.

Mystic Reg *(tearfully to audience)* I always cry at weddings.

Reg blows his nose noisily.

Friar Tuck And do you, Lady Marian Fitzwater Fitzpatrick Fitzgerald Beyonce Fitzsimmons, take this man to be your lawfully, wedded husband?

Sheriff Yes, she does, now get on with it!!

Friar Tuck Then by the power vested in me, I pronounce you...

Enter Robin Hood, clutching a sword.

Robin Wait! This wedding shall not continue!

Maid Marian Robin!

Mystic Reg *(To audience)* I didn't see that coming.

Sheriff *(through angry gritted teeth)* Robin Hood!!! How did you get out of jail?

Robin You underestimate me, sir!

At that moment, some of the villagers remove their capes and hoods to reveal that they are Dame Dora, Will Scarlett, Little June, Alan a Dale, and Juliet. They all draw swords and point them at the castle guards

The Sheriff draws his sword and lunges towards Robin.

Sheriff Defend yourself Robin Hood. I shall finish you once and for all!

Robin I am not afraid of you, Sheriff. Do your worst!

A furious sword fight takes place. The advantage swings back and forth until finally Robin knocks the Sheriff's sword out of his hand and pins his adversary to the ground with the tip of his own sword.

Robin The game's up Sheriff. I think you'll find that it is *you* that is going to be arrested.

Sheriff I don't understand. How did your men get past the castle guards.
Robin Let's just say they had a little help from a very special friend.

King Richard enters accompanied by Long Face the horse.

First Castle Guard It's King Richard!

Marion Father!

Second Castle Guard The king has returned!

Sheriff Your majesty?

King Richard *(To the guards)* By royal decree, I order the castle guards to lay down their arms!

The guards all throw their swords onto the floor.

All God save the King! God save the King!

Sheriff *(to audience)* Well, this has turned out to be a completely rubbish wedding day.

King Richard *(To the Sheriff)* Robin's men have informed me of the terrible wrongs you have committed in my kingdom.

Sheriff It's all lies! The people of Nottingham love me.

All Booooooo!

King Richard I think that reaction tells a different story. Not one person has stepped forward to vouch for you.

Sheriff I demand a recount!

King Richard I have little choice but to sentence you to rot in the dungeons of Nottingham Castle forever!

All Hoorah!

Sheriff Please, your Majesty! Show me mercy!

King Richard Take him away!

Two castle guards drag the Sheriff off stage.

Sheriff No! Please! Anything but the dungeons! I'm claustrophobic. I'm allergic to rats! I'm afraid of the dark…

Robin crosses to the king. Marian comes and takes his hand.

Robin Your Majesty, before you left the country I meant to ask for the hand of your beautiful daughter…

King Richard Just her hand?

Robin No! Obviously the rest of her as well.

King Richard Robin, you are a brave and true man. Nottingham owes you a great debt.

Robin Thank you, your majesty.

King Richard However, I can only let a man of noble blood marry my daughter.

Robin Oh.

Marian Father?

King Richard So, therefore, kneel Robin…

Robin Your majesty?

Robin kneels before Richard. The king touches both of Robin's shoulders with his sword, knighting him.

King Richard Arise, Sir Robin of Loxley.

Friar Tuck *(whispers)* Loxley? Where's Loxley?

Alan a Dale *(whispers)* It's just off the A61.

Friar Tuck *(whispers)* Oh.

Will Scarlett Three cheers for Sir Robin! Hip, hip, hooray! Hip, hip, hooray! Hip, hip, hooray!

Everyone cheers. Robin crosses to Marian and goes down on one knee again.

Robin Marian, will you make me the happiest man in the whole world and agree to become my wife?

Maid Marian Of course I will!

Robin and Marian embrace.

All Hooray!

Juliet kneels before Will Scarlett.

Juliet And will you make me the happiest girl in the world, Will Scarlett?

Will Scarlett Aren't I supposed to do the kneeling?

Juliet I'm a very modern woman, Will. What's your answer?

Will Scarlett Yes, of course I'll marry you!

Juliet and Will Scarlett embrace.

All Hooray!

Denchman the Henchman is standing next to Dame Dora.

Dame Dora So, Denchman the Henchman.

Denchman the Henchman Dame Dora?

Dame Dora Now that the Sheriff is where he belongs in jail, I suppose he will not be needing a henchman anymore.

Denchman the Henchman I suppose not.

Dame Dora Would you be interested in a job at my bakery? I need someone to make the holes in the doughnuts.

Denchman the Henchman Well, I'm not expecting any other job offers.

Dame Dora It's a residential position.

Denchman the Henchman Is it?

Dame Dora And if you're going to live at the bakery, we might as well get married.

Denchman the Henchman Married? But Dame Dora, I…

Dame Dora Of course, I could always ask my son's future father-in-law King Richard to throw you into the dungeons along with your boss.

Denchman takes Dame Dora's hand and kisses it.

Denchman the Henchman In that case, it would be a honour to marry you Dame Dora.

Dame Dora *(To the audience)* Ooh goody, a *triple* wedding!

King Richard And now, by order of the King of England, let's dance!

All Hooray!

Music kicks in. Everyone dances. The curtain slowly closes.

Alan a Dale, Friar Tuck and Long Face the Horse enter on tabs.

Friar Tuck Oh, I do love a happy ending.

Alan a Dale Robin's marrying Marian.

Friar Tuck Will Scarlett is marrying Juliet.

Alan a Dale Denchman the Henchman is marrying Dame Dora. For some reason.

Friar Tuck And you're *all* invited to the wedding.

All Hooray!

Friar Tuck And while we're waiting for everyone to change into their wedding outfits, we thought you'd like to sing a song with us.

Alan a Dale Would you like to sing a song with us boys and girls?

Audience Yes!

Friar Tuck Alan, go and get the words.

Alan a Dale The words?

Friar Tuck The words of the song.

Alan a Dale I know the words of the song.

Friar Tuck Yes, but the boys and girls might not know the words of the song.

Alan a Dale *(To Long Face)* Long Face, do you know the words of the song?

Long Face Neigh!

Alan a Dale *(To audience)* I really must teach that horse some more words.

Long Face Good idea.
Alan a Dale What did you say?

Long Face Nothing.

Alan a Dale You know the words of the song, don't you boys and girls?

Friar Tuck Alan, how can the boys and girls have any idea if they know the words to the song, if they don't know what song we're going to sing?

Alan a Dale I'll go and get the words.

Friar Tuck Good man.

Alan a Dale brings on a big board with the words of the song on it. Alan a Dale and Friar Tuck teach the to the audience. Long Face the Horse dances around while everyone's singing.

Song 16

At the end of the song the curtains open for the big finale and walk down.

Scene 6

Order of walk downs:
1) *Adult Ensemble.*
2) *Children Ensemble.*
3) *King Richard & Long Face the Horse.*
4) *Alan a Dale, Friar Tuck, Little June.*
5) *The Sheriff & Mystic Reg*
6) *Will Scarlett & Juliet*
7) *Dame Dora & Denchman the Henchman*
8) *Robin and Marian*

Song 17

Blackout. Curtain.

THE END

MUSICAL ITEM SUGGESTIONS

Song 1 – The Company
Wake up Boo - The Boo Radleys
I Gotta Feelin - Black Eyed Peas
Reach - S Club 7

Song 2 – Marian & Juliet
You Got a Friend in Me – Randy Newman
That's What Friends Are For - Dionne Warwick

Song 3 – Dame Dora
I'm Too Sexy – Right Said Fred
Working Nine to Five - Dolly Parton
It's Raining Men – Weather Girls

Song 4 – Friar Tuck, Little June, Will Scarlett
Together Wherever We Go – Gypsy
Count on Me – Bruno Mars
Busy Doing Nothing – Bing Crosby

Song 5 – The Sheriff & Marian
Bad Boys - Alexandra Burke
Help Yourself - Tom Jones
I Want to Break Free - Queen

Song 6 – Alan a Dale
I Would Walk Five Hundred Miles - The Proclaimers
A Million Love Songs - Take That
The Longest Time - Billy Joel

Song 7 - Juliet
It Must Be Love - Labi Siffre
It's A Kind of Magic - Queen

Song 8 – The Sheriff, Denchman & Mystic Reg
Bad Moon Rising - Credence Clearwater Revival
Bad Guys - Bugsy Malone
One Way or Another - Blondie

Song 9 – Robin & the Merry Men/Women
Men in Tights - Robin Hood, Men in Tights
We Go Together – Grease
Can't Stop the Beat - Hairspray

Song 10 – The Company
Everybody Needs Somebody - Blues Brothers
Oom, Pah, Pah! - Oliver
Light Up/Run - Snow Patrol

Song 11 – Merry Men/Women
Beat Again – JLS
Our House – Madness
Holding Out for a Hero - Bonnie Tyler

Song 12 – Will Scarlett & Juliet
Daydream Believer - Neil Diamond
Getting to Know You - Rogers and Hammerstein
Somethin' Stupid – Frank Sinatra & Nancy Sinatra

Song 13 – Robin & Marion
Everything I Do - Bryan Adams
Up Where We Belong - Joe Cocker

Song 14 - Dame Dora, Juliet, Will & the Ghosts
Ghostbusters – Ray Parker Jr.
Monster Mash – Bobby Pickett
Thriller – Michael Jackson
Bad Moon Rising - Credence Clearwater Revival

Song 15 - Marian
I Will Always Love You – Whitney Houston
Someone Like You – Adele
The Show Must Go On – Queen
I'll Always Have You – Colin Blunstone

Song 16 - Alan a Dale & Friar Tuck
One Finger One Thumb
I am the Music Man
Always Look on the Bright Side
Old MacDonald

Song 17 – The Company
Happy - Pharrell Williams
Live While We're Young - One Direction
The Best Song Ever - One Direction
Celebration by Kool and the Gang

About the author

Brian Luff's animated comedy shows *Monday Tuesday Banana* and *Space Planet* won awards at the Lisbon Film Festival and at the Prague International Film Festival in 2020.

Brian co-wrote the cult Channel 4 comedy series *Pets* and was a commissioned writer on Simon Pegg's Channel 5 sketch shows *Six Pairs of Pants* and *We Know Where You Live*.

On the Edinburgh Fringe, Brian has co-written and co-produced numerous sketch shows and penned a full length stage comedy *The Moon's Not a Virgin Anymore*. He has also edited the official BBC comedy web site and has been a visiting lecturer in comedy writing at Bournemouth University.

For more pantomime scripts by Brian Luff go to pantoscripts.biz

Printed in Great Britain
by Amazon